S0-BAS-311

The Case of the Drooling Dinosaurs

Tommy Nelson® Books by Bill Myers

Series

SECRET AGENT DINGLEDORF
. . . and his trusty dog, SPLAT 🐾

The Case of the Giggling Geeks
The Case of the Chewable Worms
The Case of the Flying Toenails
The Case of the Drooling Dinosaurs
The Case of the Hiccupping Ears

The Incredible Worlds of
Wally McDoogle

—*My Life As a Smashed Burrito with Extra Hot Sauce*
—*My Life As Alien Monster Bait*
—*My Life As a Broken Bungee Cord*
—*My Life As Crocodile Junk Food*
—*My Life As Dinosaur Dental Floss*
—*My Life As a Torpedo Test Target*
—*My Life As a Human Hockey Puck*
—*My Life As an Afterthought Astronaut*
—*My Life As Reindeer Road Kill*
—*My Life As a Toasted Time Traveler*
—*My Life As Polluted Pond Scum*
—*My Life As a Bigfoot Breath Mint*
—*My Life As a Blundering Ballerina*
—*My Life As a Screaming Skydiver*
—*My Life As a Human Hairball*
—*My Life As a Walrus Whoopee Cushion*
—*My Life As a Computer Cockroach (Mixed-Up Millennium Bug)*
—*My Life As a Beat-Up Basketball Backboard*
—*My Life As a Cowboy Cowpie*
—*My Life As Invisible Intestines with Intense Indigestion*
—*My Life As a Skysurfing Skateboarder*
—*My Life As a Tarantula Toe Tickler*

Picture Book
Baseball for Breakfast

www.Billmyers.com

SECRET AGENT DINGLEDORF

... and his trusty dog, SPLAT

The Case of the Drooling Dinosaurs

BILL MYERS

Illustrations
Meredith Johnson

Tommy
NELSON®

www.tommynelson.com

A Division of Thomas Nelson, Inc.
www.ThomasNelson.com

Text copyright © 2003 by Bill Myers
Illustrations by Meredith Johnson. Copyright © 2003 by Tommy
Nelson®, a Division of Thomas Nelson, Inc.

All rights reserved. No portion of this book may be reproduced
in any form without the written permission of the publisher,
with the exception of brief excerpts in reviews.

Published in Nashville, Tennessee, by Tommy Nelson®, a Division
of Thomas Nelson, Inc.

Scripture quotations marked (NLT) are taken from the *Holy
Bible,* New Living Translation, copyright © 1996. Used by permission of Tyndale House Publishers, Inc., Wheaton, Illinois
60189. All rights reserved.

Library of Congress Cataloging-in-Publication Data

Myers, Bill, 1953–
    The case of the drooling dinosaurs / Bill Myers ; illustra-
tions, Meredith Johnson.
        p. cm.—(Secret Agent Dingledorf . . . and his trusty dog,
    Splat ; 4)
    Summary: Ten-year-old Secret Agent Dingledorf learns the
value of following the rules when he reluctantly faces Dr.
Rebellion, a man who is causing chaos all over town because
he hates rules.
    ISBN: 1-4003-0177-7 (pbk.)
    [1. Rules (Philosophy)—Fiction. 2. Behavior—Fiction. 3.
Spies—Fiction. 4. Humorous stories.] I. Johnson, Meredith,
ill. II. Title.
PZ7.M98234 Can 2003
[Fic]—dc22   2003015481

Printed in the United States of America

03 04 05 06 07 PHX 6 5 4 3 2

To Beverly Phillips—
for all these years
she's put up with us!

*"For the Lord's sake,
accept all authority—"*

1 Peter 2:13 (NLT)

Contents

CHAPTER 1

The Case Begins . . .

I raced to school with my best friend I.Q., the human computer. Well, I raced. I.Q. did a lot more tripping over his shoes

"AHHH!"

than racing.

The only thing greater than I.Q.'s brains is his clumsiness. I mean, the guy is worse than my cousin Wally McDoogle. Well, not that bad. (Nobody can be that bad.) But he's close.

"Bernie!" He sniffed. "What's the hurry?"

(I.Q. always sniffs. He's allergic to everything . . . except being clumsy.)

"My science report is today!" I shouted as I helped him to his feet. "I've got to hurry and set it up!"

We arrived at the street corner across from the school. I started to cross, but I.Q. grabbed me. "We have to wait for the *(sniff-sniff)* crossing guard!"

He was right, but I was in a hurry.

Instead of waiting, I ran across the street, dragging him with me.

No problem. Well, except for his screaming:

"WE'RE GOING TO *(sniff-sniff)* GET HIT!"

and our almost

Honk! Honk!

SQUEEEEEEEEAAL . . .

getting hit.

Fortunately, the car missed us.

Unfortunately, the driver of the car wasn't happy. "You could have been hit!" he yelled.

"Told you." I.Q. sniffed.

The crossing guard was also mad. "You're supposed to follow the rules," she shouted. "You could have been hit."

You'd think I'd get the message (especially the part about getting hit). But I had more important things to do than follow their rules. Besides, what does breaking a few rules hurt?

Unfortunately, I was about to find out.

A few minutes later, I stood in front of Mrs. Hooplesnort's class. I was giving my report on dinosaurs. It was pretty cool. I used a bunch of little toy dinosaurs and pretended they were attacking each other.

I said, "These bigger dino boys would eat these little dino guys . . ."

chomp, chomp

"Who would eat these littler guys . . ."

munch, munch

"Who would eat these littlest guys . . ."

crunch, crunch
BURP!

(Hey, what fun is it giving reports without

sound effects?)

When I finished, I asked, "Are there any questions?"

Priscilla, my other best friend, raised her hand. She's a girl, but doesn't like anybody to mention it. The fact that she can beat up anyone who reminds her helps everybody to forget.

"Yes?" I said.

"How do you make them do that?" she asked.

"Do what?"

"How do you make them run all around the table like that . . . and jump onto the floor like that . . . AND . . . SCAMPER UNDER OUR FEET LIKE—"

"EEEK AKKK AWWWK!"

If you guessed that was some of the

kids yelling, your guesser guessed right.

Everyone was jumping up on their desks and screaming their lungs out.

The reason?

My dino guys were attacking each other just like I showed. Except for one minor detail . . .

Now, they were doing it all by—

chomp, chomp
munch, munch
crunch, crunch
BURP!

themselves!

CHAPTER 2

Big Guy Says, "Hi!"

So, everybody was standing on their desks screaming when, suddenly, . . .

beep-beep-beep-beep

my underwear started ringing.

I lowered my head and shouted, "Hello?!"

"Secret Agent Dingledorf?" It was Big Guy, head of our secret agency. He and everybody else in the government think I'm some sort of agent. I've tried to explain they're wrong. But my accidentally solving all of their cases doesn't help.

"Big Guy?!" I asked.

"Are your toy dinosaurs coming to life?" he shouted.

"How did you know?"

"A machine is making dinosaurs all around the city come to life. Big ones, little ones—even the skeletons at the museum! We need your help!"

"What can I do?"

"Grab that wad of used chewing gum under your desk!"

"What?!" I yelled. "That's gross!!"

"It's not really gum. It's . . .

hiss-hiss
crackle-crackle

. . . so just add water."

"What?" I shouted. "You're breaking up. I can't hear you!"

"I said, I'll be there soon. Just add water to that gum and ..."

crackle-crackle
hiss-hiss

"Hello?" I shouted. "Hello, Big Guy? Can you hear me?!"

But it was no good. We were cut off.

I looked around the room. By now my dino dudes were really going at it. Not only were they fighting, now they were also drooling. Oh, and one other thing: They weren't just attacking each other. A few were climbing up students' desks and

chomp, chomp-ing
munch, munch-ing
drool, drool-ing

on the kids, which led to even more

"EEEK   AKKK   AWWWK"-ing

and fainting.

K-thud

Lots and lots of

K-thud, K-thud, K-thud

fainting.

Now, to be honest, I wasn't crazy about grabbing someone's used gum. But things were getting pretty noisy from all that screaming and fainting. And Big Guy had never lied to me before (except when he wasn't telling the truth). So . . .

I reached under the desk. A huge wad of something was stuck there.

(Eewww!)

I grabbed it and pulled.

(Double *Eewww!*)

It was pink and stringy and gooey. Just like real gum.

The only difference was, it had tiny little instructions printed on its side. Tiny little instructions that read:

Just add water.

Unfortunately, the water fountain was out in the hallway. And since the floor was still covered with dining dinos, and since I didn't want them dining on my tootsies, I had to think of something else.

Luckily, their drool gave me an idea.

I knelt down on my desk. I put the gum in my hand and slowly lowered it to the floor.

One of the critters spotted it. It must have been in the mood for a finger sandwich because it raced toward my pinkies, drooling all the way.

Luckily, its drool hit the gum before its jaws hit my fingers.

Suddenly, . . .

K-BOOM!

the little wad of gum turned into a giant, jet-powered backpack!

Not only that, but its engines were already

VAA-RRROOOOM-ing.

Talk about scary.

Fortunately, everyone had quit screaming.

Unfortunately, it was because they'd all

K-thud, K-thud, K-thud

fainted.

Everyone except Mrs. Hooplesnort.

"Bernard Dingledorf!" she shouted as she tap-danced on her desk to keep the dinos from munching on her toes. "You know better than to bring jet-powered backpacks to class!"

Before I could explain, Big Guy appeared outside our third-story window. He was hovering in a jet-pack exactly like mine.

In his arms he held Splat, my brave and fearless Wonder-dog. (Though he might have looked braver and more fearless if he wasn't covering his eyes and whimpering in terror.)

Big Guy motioned for me to slip on my jet-pack.

I did.

He pointed to a big green button on the side. Next to it was some writing that read:

WARNING

Press only if you want to fly out of rooms.

I pressed it, and

VAA-RRROOOOM

shot into the air.

That was the good news.

Unfortunately, there was a little bad news. And it sounded like:

K-RASH!
tinkle, tinkle, tinkle!

(which, of course, is the sound windows make when someone wearing a jet-pack flies through them).

At least I was outside.

The only problem was, nobody told me how to control the thing.

One minute I was flying sideways.

"WAHHH!"

Then upside down.

"WHOA!"

Then spinning around and around like a windmill gone crazy.

"WOO-WOO-WOO-WOO!"

Unfortunately, that wasn't nearly as bad as what was next. . . .

CHAPTER 3

Big Guy Says, "Bye!"

So, there I was, flying around in an out-of-control jet-pack like . . . well, like some kid flying around in an out-of-control jet-pack!

Big Guy moved in to help. But his fingers barely touched my pack before he pulled away.

"Gross!" he yelled. "You've got dino drool all over your pack!"

"Sorry," I shouted. "It was the only liquid I could find!"

"But dino drool means dino germs!"

"So?"

He gave a shudder. "So, I hate germs."

"Since when?"

"Since Splat flushed us down the toilet in *The Case of the Chewable Worms*!"

"Sorry!"

"Not as sorry as you'll be solving this case on your own!"

Suddenly, Big Guy shoved the trembling Wonder-dog into my hands and turned on his jet-power pack to leave.

"Where are you going?" I shouted.

"To wash and shower and scrub and bathe."

"And after that?"

"Then bathe and scrub and shower and wash."

"But you're supposed to help me!"

He didn't answer. Instead, he

VAA-RRROOOOM-ed

away faster than my oldest sister dumped her last boyfriend.

I shouted after him, "Don't forget to wash behind your ears!" But I doubt he heard.

If he did, he didn't answer. Well, maybe he did. It's hard to hear anything when you're still busy

"WAAA!"
"WHOA!"
and
"WOO-WOO-WOO-WOO!"-ing

all over the sky.

Luckily, Splat was there to help. He might have helped more if he hadn't climbed up to my face and wrapped his pudgy paws around it.

"Mwatt, mwet go!" I shouted. "Mwatt, mwet go!"

(*Translation:* "Splat, let go! Splat, let go!")

But he didn't hear. It's hard to hear anything when you're busy whimpering for your life.

Good ol' Splat. (If he were any more chicken, he'd be sprouting feathers.)

Still, with all of his kicking, whimpering (and clucking), his back paws accidentally hit another little button that read:

WARNING

Press only if you want to fly to Headquarters.

We took off faster than Dad grabs the TV remote from us.

Headquarters is on an island so secret that it's guarded day and night by all sorts of fighter jets and missiles. That's the good news.

The bad news is, nobody bothered to

tell the jet fighters with their missiles that we were coming.

No problem, except for the part where the missiles started

zing, zing, zing-ing

at us. And the fighter jets started

K-woosh, K-woosh, K-woosh-ing

past us.

Luckily, we were still

"WAAA!"
"WHOA!"
and
"WOO-WOO-WOO-WOO!"-ing

around so much that they couldn't hit us.

Unluckily, we were

"WAAA!"
"WHOA!"
and
"WOO-WOO-WOO-WOO!"-ing

around so much that when we finally

K-RASH-ed

onto the beach, we were pretty sick.

In fact, we were so sick, all we could do was drop to our knees, lean over, and . . .

(WARNING: This sound effect has been censored. You'll just have to use your imagination.)

Then I heard a voice. "Secret Agent Dingledorf?"

I spun around, but nobody was there. In fact, the only thing on the beach was a small ivy plant.

"Secret Agent Dingledorf?"

"Who's talking?" I asked.

"Me."

"Me, who?"

"Me, the plant."

"No way!" I shouted. I bent down for a better look. "You're a plant?"

"Actually, I'm a robot disguised as a plant. Now, please, the world is being destroyed, and you're the only one who can save it!"

I still didn't believe my eyes . . . or my ears. I reached out to touch a leaf. That's when the vine grabbed my arm and flipped me onto my back.

"Aiii-YAAAA!"

When I came to, I groaned. "How did you do that?"

"Three years of karate lessons," the plant said. "Now, follow me!"

Suddenly, it shot out another vine

slither-slither-slither

across the sand.

"Hurry!" it shouted. "We haven't much time!"

I glanced at Splat, who was doing what he does best—shaking and whimpering.

It looked like fun and I would have joined him, but there was still that minor little problem. You know, the one about being the only person who can save the world.

It's a lousy job, but somebody has to do it.

So, with a heavy sigh, I followed the talking plant, or robot, or whatever it was.

CHAPTER 4

Headquarters

We followed the vine to the usual secret agent elevator built into the usual secret agent mountain.

We climbed on board and fell the usual

"AAAUGHhhhh ..."

3,000 feet to Headquarters.

It was just as I remembered. People were running all over the place like shoppers at a Christmas sale. (But without all the screaming and fistfights.) An agent grabbed my jet-powered backpack.

Every wall had TV screens even bigger than the ones at the mall Dad dreams about.

"Secret Agent Dingledorf?"

I spun around to see my plant pal. The little vine had grown into a full bush.

"Wow!" I yelled. "My mom would love to know what plant food you use!"

"I'm Ivy, Big Guy's assistant."

"You're in charge now?"

"While he is away."

"Listen," I coughed nervously. "I'm not so sure I want to take orders from a, you know."

"From an assistant?" she asked.

"Well, no, actually, I mean from . . . uh, you know, a talking plant."

"I told you, I'm a robot. Do you have something against talking robots?"

"Well, no, but—"

"Good, because I have nothing against talking humans. Now, can we get back to saving the world?"

"Well, okay. . . ."

She pointed a trembling leaf at one of the TV screens. On it was a bunch of giant dinosaur skeletons. They were running down the street, stomping on cars, slobbering on folks' heads, and being just plain rude.

"Where did they come from?" I asked.

"The local museum."

She pointed to another screen. On it were smaller toy dinos. They were doing their own version of stomping, drooling, and rudeness.

"These are from the local toy stores."

"I don't understand," she said.

She explained. "Every dino of every shape, color, and size has come to life."

"But how?" I asked. "Who could do such a thing?"

The plant pointed to another screen.

On it was an old man with a green Mohawk.

"His name is Dr. Rebellion," the plant said. "He owns the local Fun Park. He wanted to visit the museum's dinosaur exhibit. But he didn't want to stand in line."

"So?"

"Dr. Rebellion hates following rules."

"What happened?"

"Since he couldn't go see the dinosaurs, he's making them come see him."

"How?"

"He is broadcasting radio waves from a computer to make them come alive."

I glanced at Splat. He gave his usual whimper.

I didn't blame him. On the Weirdness Scale of 1 to 10, this was pushing a 12.

Miss Ivy continued. "He is hiding out at his Fun Park. If the dinosaurs go there, thousands of people will be trampled to death."

"How will we stop him?" I asked.

"We won't."

"We won't?"

"We won't."

"Who will?"

"You will."

I shook my head. "No way."

"Yes way."

"How way?"

"This way." The plant shot another vine out at Splat and me.

It wrapped around our legs tighter than the jeans Dad won't let my sisters wear in public.

Of course, we fought like heroes—kicking, screaming, and hollering for our mommies. But it made no difference.

Miss Ivy's new vine dragged us all the way to the Gizmo Lab.

The lab had really changed since my last visit. Now it was a zoo.

Literally!

"What did you do to it?" I yelled.

"Big Guy let me make a few changes."

"I liked the old way," I complained.

"Where are the cool gizmos?"

"You're looking at them."

I shook my head. "All I see are plants and animals and stuff."

"Now everything is made from nature."

I frowned. "Nature gizmos? What good are nature gizmo—"

"LOOK OUT!"

We ducked just as a jet-powered pine-apple

WHOOOSH-ed

past our heads and

K-Splat-ed

on the wall behind us!

Next, I spotted a bunch of barefoot

scientists. They were inching their way toward us.

"What are they doing?" I asked.

"Looking for where they planted an invisible thorn patch."

Suddenly, they started jumping up and down.

"OUCH! OUCH! OOOUUCH!"

"Looks like they found it," she said.

MOOOO!
MOOOO!
MOOOO!

I looked up just in time to see a herd of cows flying over our heads. On each of their backs sat a chicken.

"What are they doing?" I yelled.

"They're our brand-new bombers."

Suddenly, a hen clucked and laid an egg. And then another clucked and laid an egg. And then another, and another, until they were all going at it.

But these weren't ordinary eggs.

Because, as they rolled off the cows' backs and fell, they . . .

ZZZZZZZzz . . .

K-BLAM!

ZZZZZZZzz . . .

K-BLAM!

"How do they explode?" I shouted.

"We put gunpowder in their . . .

ZZZZZZzz . . .
K-BLAM!

food!"

It was pretty impressive. Well, except for the giant holes they left in the floor.

"How's this going to stop the dinosaurs?" I shouted.

Suddenly, an alarm sounded with all sorts of flashing lights and beepers.

"WHAT'S THAT?!" I yelled.

"IT'S THE DINO DIGEST ALARM!" Miss Ivy shouted.

"THE WHAT?!"

"IT MEANS THEY'RE ABOUT TO START DIGESTING!"

"DIGESTING?" I yelled.

"HURRY!" the plant shouted. She shoved a new backpack into my hands.

"WHAT'S THIS?"

"YOUR NATURE GIZMOS!"

"MY WHAT?"

"MAKE SURE YOU FOLLOW THE INSTRUCTIONS! AND NO STOPPING. GO STRAIGHT TO THE FUN PARK!"

"BUT—"

"HURRY, THEY'RE ABOUT TO DIGEST!"

"DIGEST WHAT?!" I shouted.

"PEOPLE!"

With that happy news, Miss Ivy sent out another vine. It wrapped around Splat and me. Then it began whipping us around the lab.

"WHOA!"

"WAAA!"

"whimper."

Suddenly, a giant door opened in the ceiling. I saw a speck of daylight far above our heads.

Miss Ivy let go and we—

"AHHHHHHHH . . ."

shot up that chute at 3½ gazillion miles an hour.

The good news was, we were definitely free of the lab and on our way.

The bad news was, I didn't know where we were going!

CHAPTER 5

The Battle Begins

Flying through the air at 3½ gazillion miles an hour wasn't so bad.

It might have been better if they'd shown us a movie on the flight.

And, it might have been best if we'd been inside a plane where they could've shown that movie.

Other than that, it was okay. Well, except for those sea gulls—

"LOOK OUT!"
K-thunk, K-thud, K-whack

that got in our way.

Splat began barking. Well, sort of.

"Mwoofth! Mwoofth!"

"What's that, boy? I can't understand you."

He tried again, but with the same results.

"Mwoofth! Mwoofth!"

(I guess it's hard barking with a mouth full of sea gull feathers.)

He pointed down to the ground.

I looked to see a dinosaur racing out of a bookstore.

I remembered what Miss Ivy had said about going straight to the Fun Park. I knew I was supposed to follow her rules. But I also wanted to investigate.

So, I broke the rules and reached into my new "nature" backpack.

The first thing I pulled out of it was a cat. On its collar were the words:

WARNING

Use only to stop flying.

"Great," I groaned. "How is some cat going to—"

Suddenly, it started clawing at the air, trying to pull us toward the ground.

"MRREEOOOW!"

Which caused Splat to start clawing at the air, trying to pull us to the cat.

"WOOF! WOOF!"

And, with all those claws clawing, we started slowing.

Then we started

"A   "M   "W
H   R   O
 H   R   O
  H   E   F
  h   e
   h   o   w
   h   o   o
    h   o   o
    h"   w"   f"

falling.

Fortunately, the cat didn't feel like giving up one of its nine lives. So it immediately changed directions and started clawing upward.

"MRREEOOOW!"

Causing Splat to start clawing upward.

"WOOF! WOOF!"

Causing us all to fall more slowly. So slowly, in fact, that we made a smooth landing in the bookstore's parking lot.

But that was only the beginning of our trouble. Why?

BECAUSE WE LANDED RIGHT IN THE MIDDLE OF THE DINOSAUR'S PATH!!!

(Sorry, didn't mean to yell.)

I leaped out of the way just as a giant dino foot came

STOMP-ing

down.

So did Splat.

I jumped up and ran between the parked cars toward the store.

So did Splat.

Well, sort of. Instead of running between parked cars, he sort of

K-Splat, K-Splat, K-Splat

ran *into* them. (At least you know how he got his name.)

I looked back over my shoulder and came to a stop. The giant dinosaur foot was made only of cardboard! Come to think of it, so was the giant dinosaur. It wasn't real at all. It was just a store display.

But that didn't stop it from running . . . and *STOMP*-ing!

Next, I heard:

clatter-clunk, clatter-clunk, clatter-clunk.

I turned toward the store's door. A bunch of videos were marching out of it.

But these weren't just any videos. No sir. These were little-kid dinosaur videos. Lots of them.

Behind the videos marched tiny, stuffed dinos.

smush-smush, smush-smush, smush-smush

They must have been from those little preschool pop-up books!

Amazing. Dr. Rebellion was bringing every dinosaur to life.

But how could I stop him?

Suddenly, I heard:

Stomp! Stomp!
K-rash!, K-rash!
"Scream! Scream!"

I figured the *Stomp*-s and *K-rash*-es were more dinosaurs on the loose.

It was the "Scream! Scream!" that worried me.

"Scream! Scream!" that sounded like kids.

"Scream! Scream!" that sounded like kids from my school just a few blocks away!

I had to get there—and fast!

I reached into my new backpack and pulled out a little jar. It had a label that read:

STORM IN A BOTTLE
Directions: Open lid for fast trips.

I wasn't sure how a jar would help.

I unscrewed the top and, suddenly,

WOOOOOOSSHHH

a giant storm cloud rushed out. It blew hard . . . so hard that I could barely stand up.

Then it began raining. It rained hard . . . so hard that I got soaked.

I reached back into the pack and rummaged around until I found an umbrella. I pulled it out and opened it.

The wind grabbed it and blew it from my hands. Luckily, it hooked onto my backpack. Unluckily, it startled Splat, causing him to jump to the top of the umbrella.

I hung on, Splat clung on—just as

WOOOOOOSSHHH

the wind picked us up and blew us into the air.

Of course, I did my usual

"AHHH!"-ing.

And, of course, Splat did his usual

"whimper, whimper"-ing.

But nothing seemed to work.
Wherever we were going, there was no
stopping us!

CHAPTER 6

More Rules

So, there we were, making like Mary Poppins with our flying umbrella.

Soon, we were over my school. That's when we saw the other dinosaurs. The big skeleton ones that had escaped from the museum.

At the moment they were busy

STOMP, STOMP, STOMP-ing

onto our school playground, while the kids were busy

"Scream! Scream! Screaming!"

inside our school building.

Well, most of the kids.

I.Q. had spotted me. He quit screaming and started shouting:

"BERNIE *(sniff-sniff)*, SAVE US!
SAVE US *(sniff-sniff)*, BERNIE!"

I had to land and help them!

I reached into my backpack for another nature gizmo. The first thing I pulled out was a snail.

"Great," I groaned. "How will a snail help us land?"

"Actually, I won't," the snail said.

"Yikes! A talking snail?!" I yelled.

"I'm not a talking snail," the talking snail said.

"You sound like a talking snail," I said.

"Look at my lips," the talking snail said.

"Do you see my lips moving?"

It was right. They weren't moving.

"Boy," I said, "for a talking snail, you're pretty talented."

"I am not a talking snail!" the talking snail said. "If I were a talking snail, then I'd be talking."

"I think I'm getting a headache," I said.

"So am I."

"I didn't know talking snails could get headaches."

"I AM NOT A TALKING SNAIL!"

"Right," I said. "You're more of a shouting snail."

"Secret Agent Dingledorf, I am speaking to you through a speaker we have attached to the snail's shell."

Suddenly, I recognized the voice. "Miss Ivy?" I yelled. "Is that you?"

"Yes," she sighed. "I'm broadcasting to

you from Headquarters."

"How do I land?" I shouted. "How do I stop and help my friends?"

"I ordered you NOT to stop. I ordered you to go straight to the Fun Park."

"Yes, but—"

"Obey my orders."

"But these dino dudes are attacking my school!"

"They are merely crossing the playground on their way to the Fun Park."

"But—"

"Secret Agent Dingledorf, you must obey my orders!"

I looked down at my school. The kids were still

"SCREAM! SCREAMING!"

And I.Q. was still

"BERNIE *(sniff-sniff)*, SAVE US!
SAVE US *(sniff-sniff)*, BERNIE!"

I turned to the snail to argue, but
Miss Ivy cut me off.

"The dinosaurs will not attack the
building," she said. "They are all going to
the Fun Park."

It was a tough decision . . . to obey my
boss, who just happened to be a talking
plant (when she wasn't a talking snail),
or to disobey and land on the playground.

I took a deep breath and made my
decision. I reached into my backpack for
something that would help me land.

But Miss Ivy would not give up.

"Remember what happened at the
bookstore?" she shouted.

"I nearly got stomped to death!"

"That's right," she yelled. "And why?"

"Why?" I said. "Well, because . . . because . . ." and then I understood. "Because I disobeyed?"

"Right! You were nearly destroyed because you didn't follow the rules!"

"But what about my friends? What about my school?"

"They will be all right. Trust me!"

I hesitated. Finally, I obeyed and pulled my hand out of the pack . . . just as the dino dudes passed the school and headed down the street.

I let out a heavy sigh. "That was close," I said.

"Follow the rules, and we will win!" Miss Ivy yelled. "It's the only way."

I nodded.

"And hurry! There's not much time!"

With that, the snail reared back its head and let out the world's biggest

"AH . . . CHOOoo!!!"

It was so loud and powerful, not to mention wet (*Eewww!*), that it shot us up the street like a rocket.

And since we had a long way to go, it kept right on

"AH . . . CHOOoo!!!"
"AH . . . CHOOoo!!!"
"AH . . . CHOOoo!!!"-ing
(while I kept right on:
"Eewww! Eewww! Eewww!"-ing.)

Finally, the Fun Park came into view.
I could see about a billion people.
The dinosaurs were a long way off but quickly approaching. I had to warn the crowd. I had to protect them.

But how?

I turned to Splat. "Now what?!" I shouted.

"Whimper, whimper," he answered.

I couldn't have agreed more.

CHAPTER 7

Dr. Rebellion

The dinos were coming from all directions . . .

—the little ones from my science project,

—the stuffed ones from the toy store,

—the video and pop-up ones from the bookstore,

—and, of course, the huge skeleton guys from the museum.

The way I figured it, the skeleton guys were the most dangerous. At least, they did the most *STOMP*-ing (and drooling). So, when we were a block from the Fun

Park gate, I spun around to fight them off.

A good idea.

Except when you fight drooling dinosaurs, it's nice to have something to fight with.

But I wasn't worried. Not in the slightest. I reached into my backpack and pulled out . . .

"A peanut!" I yelled. "How am I going to fight off dinosaurs with a peanut?!"

I tried not to panic.

Maybe it was like a special ray gun. *Yeah, that was it!* I pointed one end at the dinos, squeezed, and . . .

Nothing.

Well, nothing except my dino pals were

STOMP, STOMP, STOMP-ing

a lot closer.

Okay, maybe it was some sort of guided missile thingy. I pointed the other end of the peanut at the dinos, squeezed, and—

More of nothing.

Well, except the dinos were

STOMP, STOMP, STOMP-ing

even closer.

I stared at the peanut in my hand . . . until a squirrel ran out of my backpack, grabbed it, ate it,

BURP!

and ran back in.

(Well, at least it was good for something.)

By now, the first dino had reached us and

ROARRRR-ed

right into my face.

(Talk about bad breath. But I guess that happens if you haven't brushed your fangs in six gazillion years!)

I couldn't fight back. I couldn't even offer it a breath mint. Suddenly, it thrust out its claw and

K-wack-ed

Splat and me.

No problem. Except its k-wacker *k-wack*-ed us down to a smaller dino. This one had a long, pointy tail. A long, pointy tail that it liked to use for a baseball bat.

Again, no problem, unless, of course, it thinks you're a baseball.

Which it did.
Which explains the sudden

K-NOCK!

Which explains Splat and me sailing high
into the air and over the Fun Park gate.

Which also explains our

"AHHHHHHHH!"
"whimper, whimper, whimper."

The first thing I knew, we hit one of the giant sails from the Pirate Ship ride.

The second thing I knew, we were sliding down that sail until we came face to face with . . .

The third thing I *DIDN'T* want to know: Dr. Rebellion.

Everything about the old man said he hated rules. Even the way he dressed.

For starters, he had on a tuxedo. But he wore the jacket as pants (with his legs sticking out of the sleeves). And he wore the pants as a jacket (with his arms sticking out of the legs).

And remember that green Mohawk he had?

Well now, it didn't run from the front to the back of his head, but across it . . . from ear to ear! He stood next to a bunch of old movie projectors. Beside them was a giant computer that he must have been using to control the dinosaurs.

I staggered to my feet. "You've got to shut that down," I shouted. "You've got to call off the dinosaurs!"

"But I want to see them," he whined.

"Then follow the rules, and stand in line at the museum!"

"But I don't want to!"

ROAR!!

stomp, stomp, stomp

The dinos were getting closer.

"You've got to follow the rules!" I shouted.

"Why?" he demanded. "Think how fun the world would be if you didn't have rules."

Before I could answer, he turned on one of the movie projectors.

It lit up a sail over our heads. In the

movie a bunch of kids were hollering, having a food fight, and watching anything they wanted on TV.

It looked like fun. Real fun.

I kept on watching. For some reason, I couldn't stop.

Dr. Rebellion's voice grew soft and smooth. "Imagine a world where you don't have to obey anyone. Where you can do anything you want."

I continued to stare at the movie. Everyone was having such a great time. Maybe Dr. Rebellion was right. Maybe—

"Don't fall for his tricks, Agent Dingledorf! He's trying to control your mind!"

It was Miss Ivy calling from my backpack.

But it didn't matter. I was already hooked on the movie.

With an evil laugh, Dr. Rebellion turned on another projector that lit up another sail.

It was even better.

Kids were pigging out at an ice-cream shop. And I do mean "pigging." You name it, they were shoving it into their snouts, er, mouths. Everyone was covered in chocolate sauce, caramel, bananas, and those little red cherries. And nobody was making them quit.

"Imagine," Dr. Rebellion whispered, "a world where you can eat whatever you want, whenever you want."

He turned to Splat, his voice even smoother. "And nobody will ever tell you to stop."

That did it for Splat. His little tail began to . . .

thump, thump, thump.

Miss Ivy continued to shout:

"Secret Agent Dingledorf!
Secret Agent Dingledorf!"

But it was obvious we'd both fallen under Dr. Rebellion's spell.

Especially Splat, who'll eat anything. Even if it's a movie shown on a sail.

Unfortunately, that's exactly what he tried to do.

He leaped up once, twice, three times— before he grabbed the bottom of the sail in his teeth. It was the part where the banana split was showing. Then he started eating it!

"Doggie, no!" Dr. Rebellion shouted.

But he was too late.

Splat may be little, but he weighs a ton. Soon the entire sail started to

RIPPP . . .

"Look what you're doing!" Dr. Rebellion shouted. "Look what you're doing!"

Luckily, all his shouting (and Splat's sail *rip*-ing) broke the spell. I was able to look away from the screen.

As I did, I saw the Fun Park around us.

Now it looked like anything but *FUN!*

CHAPTER 8

The Case Closes

The Fun Park was total chaos.

But it wasn't because of the dinosaurs!

Oh, sure, they were getting closer and closer. And they were doing their usual

STOMP, STOMP, STOMP-ing
and
drool, drool, drool-ing.

But now that the sail was ripped away, I finally saw the people. They were busy fighting and crowding in front of each other, trying to be next on the rides. No one waited their turn. Instead, everyone was taking cuts as they punched and screamed and hit and hollered!

Dr. Rebellion finally saw them, too. "STOP IT!" he shouted over the noise. "WHAT ARE YOU DOING?! STOP IT AT ONCE!"

"We don't have to!" someone yelled.

"Why not?" he shouted.

"Because of the sign you made!" they yelled.

They all pointed to a sign that read:

RULES:

There are none.

"But this isn't right!" he shouted.

I turned to him and yelled, "They're just doing what you want!"

"But . . . I wanted them to have fun!" he shouted. "Not this!"

A kid who had just eaten five cotton

candies, four corn dogs, and a giant spinach pizza staggered in front of us.

For obvious reasons, he looked pretty sick.

He sounded even sicker when he dropped to his knees and:

(Imagine the same censored sound
effect you did on page 25.)

"This is terrible!" Dr. Rebellion said.

"LOOK!" I yelled.

We jumped to the side as a bumper car smashed into the crowd. (Talk about reckless . . . the driving was almost as bad as my oldest sister's driving.)

BEEP, BEEP
K-rash!

(Almost.)

"Get that bumper car back on its track!" Dr. Rebellion shouted.

But the driver just laughed. He pointed to the sign. Then he zoomed off, hitting as many things and people as he could.

Suddenly, . . .

STOMP—drool
STOMP—drool
STOMP—drool

(If you guessed the dinos had finally reached the park's gate, you guessed right.)

"Don't you get it?!" I shouted at Dr. Rebellion. "If nobody follows rules, then everything will be crazy!"

He shook his head. "It's supposed to be fun. It's supposed to—"

"HELP ME! HELP ME!"

We turned to see the merry-go-round.

RULE
There
are
NONE!

TRASH

Only now, it didn't look so "merry." Someone had turned the speed to *Extra Fast*. Now the people spun around faster than the time Splat got caught in the dryer!

And then:

SCRAAAAAAPE!

"WATCH IT!"

We leaped aside just as a roller coaster VAA-RRROOOOM-ed by. A roller coaster that was no longer on its rails!

"Don't you see?!" I shouted. "You need rules!"

"But—"

K-RASH!

The dinos broke through the gate and stormed into the park.

Everyone started shouting and screaming as the dino dudes continued their

STOMP, STOMP, STOMP-ing
and
drool, drool, drool-ing.

"What do I do?!" the doctor shouted. "What do I do?!"

"Turn off the computer!" I yelled. "We've got to stop the dinos!"

He spun to the computer. He began switching switches, dialing dials, and knobbing knobs.

It was close. But just before the dinosaurs started tap-dancing on folks' heads, he shut down the computer.

Eeerrrr-kkkkk...

Suddenly, every dinosaur came to a stop. But that was only half the battle.

"Now what?" Dr. Rebellion shouted.

I looked around. Things were still crazy. But at least nobody was getting stomped (or drooled) to death.

Punched, kicked, and run over by out-of-control rides, yes—but not stomped or drooled on.

"You've got to give these people rules again!" I shouted.

He nodded his head. "I'm afraid you're right!" he yelled.

Burp!

We twirled around to see Splat.

He didn't look so good.

The reason was simple: The movie

projector was still projecting movies of food on the torn sail.

Which meant Splat was still trying to eat the torn sail.

Which meant—

"I think we better get him to a vet before . . ."

"Before what?" Dr. Rebellion yelled.

"Before he winds up making the same censored sounds that are on page 25 and page 76."

"Right!"

The two of us started running around, trying to catch the little guy.

"Here, boy! Come on, fella!"

But Splat didn't want to be caught. There was just too much "food" to eat. (Even though it tasted a lot like pirate ship sails.)

It was good to be working side by side with the doctor. It was even better to see that he had finally learned his lesson.

Come to think of it, so had I.

Obeying rules can really be important.

Now, if we could just catch Splat before he—

(WARNING: Here's that same censored
sound effect again.)

Uh, never mind.

The next day I.Q. and I headed back to school.

It was raining really hard when we arrived at the corner across the street.

Suddenly, . . .

beep-beep-beep-beep

my underwear started ringing.

Before I could answer it, the crossing guard waved us forward.

beep-beep-beep-beep

I.Q. pushed up his glasses and asked, "Aren't you *(sniff, sniff)* going to answer that?"

The crossing guard kept waving us forward. I stepped off the curb and turned to I.Q. "I'll answer it as soon as we obey the guard."

beep-beep-beep-beep

"Excuse me, son?" the crossing guard said as we passed. "I believe that's your underwear ringing."

I immediately recognized the voice and spun around to him. "Big Guy!" I yelled. "You're back!"

"Shh." He glanced around. "I'm under-cover today."

"Why aren't you at Headquarters?" I whispered.

"This is my punishment for disobeying yesterday's orders."

beep-beep-beep-beep

"Punishment?" I asked.

He nodded. "I left you without getting permission from Headquarters."

"You didn't follow the rules?" I asked.

He nodded. "Now I have to work out in the rain all day."

"So even important hotshots like you have to obey rules?" I asked.

"That's right. Tomorrow, I'll be back at my desk where it's nice and dry. But until then—"

beep-beep-beep-beep

He cleared his throat. "Until then, move across the street, young man. Then you can answer your underwear!"

I giggled.

"That's an order, Agent Dingledorf."

"Yes, sir!" I grinned.

I.Q. and I quickly crossed the street. After all, Big Guy was still my boss, and I had definitely learned the importance of obeying the

beep-beep-beep-beep

rules.

Look for These Other Books in This Series

The Case of the Giggling Geeks

The world's smartest people can't stop laughing. Is this the work of the crazy criminal Dr. Chuckles? Only Secret Agent Dingledorf (the country's greatest agent, even though he is just ten years old) can find out. Together, with super cool inventions (that always backfire), major mix-ups (that become major mishaps), and the help of Splat the Wonder-dog, our hero winds up saving the day . . . while discovering the importance of respecting and loving others.

ISBN 1-4003-0094-0

www.tommynelson.com

A Division of Thomas Nelson, Inc.
www.ThomasNelson.com

The Case of the Flying Toenails

It started out with just one little lie. But soon, everybody is coming down with the dreaded disease—Priscilla, parents, even Super-dud, er, Super-dog, Splat. They go to bed perfectly normal one night, then wake up the next morning with jet-powered toenails! Who knows the truth behind this awful sickness? Who can stop it? Only Secret Agent Dingledorf and his not-so-trusty (at least in this book) sidekick Splat can find the cure and save the day . . . while learning how important it is to always be honest and always tell the truth.

ISBN 1-4003-0096-7

Tommy NELSON®

www.tommynelson.com

A Division of Thomas Nelson, Inc.
www.ThomasNelson.com